The House On B[1]

The House On Black Hill

*This book I dedicate it to my lovely parents :
Valentina & Ion. Always love*

The House On Black Hill

The <u>grudge</u> is not in the <u>house</u>...
The <u>house</u> is the <u>grudge</u>...

The House On Black Hill

Copyright © Denisa Ditoiu

Copyright © The House on Black Hill

All right reserved.

All characters, names and facts are fictitious. And any resemblance to actual persons, living or dead, is purely coincidental.
Some names or locations have been changed for the purpose of the book.

April 2021

The House On Black Hill

The house on Black hill

Denisa's P.O.V.

Chapter 1 – The old man

" Joshua, hurry up please. We'll be late for supper and we have to take the dog back to your parents" I shout as I raise my head from the phone's screen. Joshua is walking in a zigzag manner on the dusty and empty path which leads to the Beacon, as if he would've drank too much. The dog kept dragging him in all directions with the desire of playing. It still has energy for a 10 years old Sheep dog.

The House On Black Hill

Joshua stops and faces me with neutral look, trying to hide his topaz eyes away from mine. The sun's golden strip lights sparkle in the ocean of his gaze. All sky is clear and its smoothness resemble a blank sheet of paper. The man shelters his face, away from the strength of the sunlight; patting his dark blonde hair and then reaching with his right hand, in the back pocket of his jeans, in search for his mobile. He grabs it trying to keep the dog calm on the leash then shouts that 5 o' clock is approaching.

We were on the top of the hills, where the view is breathtaking. A border of trees separates the curved path of the deserted field from the sea of greenness. An explosion of gold color and shades of green are battling with the cool breeze of the spring, mixing together harmoniously. Joshua appeared to me small in the distance, although he is much taller than myself. My forehead reaches his collarbone.

I look once more at my phone without realizing it has already passed 5. I notice my blurred reflection : messed brown hair , big brown eyes , pronounced lips and round chin. Joshua has pleasant features, though I admit I ran away in my teens from blonde guys. His nose was considerable wide, balanced by the pink thick lips. The color of his skin remained me of clean sheets, so pure and white. As soon as he realises it is getting late he comes closer at a fast pace with the dog in front of him.

" Denisa is just gone 5. Why didn't you tell me, baby?"

" You were too busy messing around with Maxwell."

Joshua remains silent just approving with a innocent smile. He sneaks his fingers between mine, glueing ours palms together. We head down to the bottom of the hill. We pass several curved trees and walked through the tall grass taking the shortcut to the Clock Tower. Our silhouettes are melting in the distance and the voice of our footsteps is swallowed by the vegetation. Somewhere nearby, a scream breaks violently the silence of the early evening. Joshua and I look at each other stunned, trying to figure out where the source of yell originates. We start to walk around, seeking for a cause of the shouting. Nothing! It took more seconds that drain like minutes when we find a figure lurking in the grass. It seems to be a man.

Joshua runs down the path, dust rising behind him. He meets a man laying in the grass. His face is wrinkled , sucked cheeks , thin lips and rough, steel-gray hair. The weeds cover his clothes and his hands shake brutally. A red stain appeared under one of his nostrils. I begin running watching the old man gasping for air. He is cold and shaken. He says he has slipped and fallen. His ankle hurts and has a start of a nosebleed. Joshua and I offered to call for help and give him our company till rescue arrives. With a husky voice, he refuses.

" I will be fine.. J-just help me stand up please if you can."

Joshua grabs the man reluctantly by the shoulders making him gather his balance. He gets up holding his stick and gathers his breath. He builds a smile as sign of gratitude. The old man wipes the blood with his tatty sleeve and introduces himself.

" You are the only people I have seen all day on the hills today. I am Jonathan Oswald. Thank you very much for your help. You are very kind."

" Not a problem mister Jonathan. Just take care next time. There are steep places around here. Do you know your way back? " asked Joshua with a note of concern in his tone.

" No, not at all. My house is just down the path on Black hill.

The House On Black Hill

It's an old retired cottage. People pass by without noticing it. You can see it better in the winter."

I examine Oswald's expression. He seems a serious man, but who is living in the middle of nowhere. We did not have any idea there was a cottage on Black hill. Perhaps a tiny one camouflaged in the woods with no electricity , stuck in time. The old man looks at me with sweet glance waiting for our reply to introduce ourselves. Although we really want to carry on and go home..

" I'm Denisa Sanders and this is my husband, Joshua. Nice to meet you."

" Lovely name, you are not from around here."

His question is intruding me, feels almost intimate. I try to smirk respectfully and avoid giving an answer. I just thank politely without bothering extending an explanation. Joshua pokes me as a sign that we should return home. It is getting late. He apologizes and wants to make a move. Jonathan Oswald insists with an invitation for a cup of tea, but we turn down his kind offer. As a final suggestion, he proposes that we should accompany him to the cottage and that is it. Joshua appeared fine with the idea. We want to make sure he doesn't fall again. Oswald starts ahead of us dragging his feet and finding support by holding the improvised stick. He begins talking about the ways the hills used to be, how people would travel to the top to grab water or have a picnic with a view over Severn Valley. I found that interesting, so kept listening with amazement.

Not long after, maybe a couple of minutes there it is – a white cottage with two brown windows that look like eyes watching us. The shape is perfectly square and the old-fashioned door gives the impression of an opened mouth. Green, messy spots here and there shows that the place is slowly falling into decay. The man is around 70 years; too old to start decorating.

He gets in the doorway and turns round half way meeting us with same grateful smile.

" You sure you don't wanna pop in for a cuppa?"

" No, thank you. We better head back. We have to drop the dog at my parents."

" Alright then. Some other time, maybe."

Joshua and I wave at him as a bye and turn round. The sound of door closing brings a relief expression on my husband's face.

" I thought we won't get away from him."

I kept my words to myself. He did not seem out of the ordinary but for a brief moment I feel cold and uneasy. Something sneaks within my essence making me shiver. A new unsafe feeling which it is not a stranger to me. I turn my head having one last glance at the cottage. In the tiny left window above the door, the sun refused to shine. But not the funny colors disturb me, nor the green stains... It is a feeling of being watched, although there is no one there...

Chapter 2 – The presence

Joshua and I head down the steep hill on the rocky path trying to make our way back to the Range Rover. Maxwell becomes increasingly agitated pulling the leash in all directions. My husband is trying to keep hold of the dog and concentrate on maintaining his own balance. He is now fighting a game of wills : his against the terrified animal.

" What's gotten into you Max?"

The dog starts to cry becoming almost hysterical. Joshua leans down and grabs Max by the head patting continuously as consolation. I have not been on many walks with him, but he usually is pretty good and quiet. Our journey to the car is never-ending. And after meeting Jonathan Oswald, it went far beyond the planed time. I grab my phone from the front pocket and realize it shows 6 o'clock. Despair is filtrating through my essence, but it is a normal feeling. It was born after we left Oswald's house. I can't shake the feeling of somebody that watched me from the petite window or...the house itself starring at me with grudge. I meditate at the idea of the man dealing with some mental health problems, hence why he rejected Joshua's suggestion to seek medical help.

Finally, we reach the Range Rover parked across the road, from a line of houses, which hid the glamour of Severn Valley. After our vehicle, there were double yellow lines and a deserted road. Typical for a Sunday afternoon.

" Damn now we are really late for tea."

" Your parents will be fine. We will tell' em what happened

and that's it!"

"That guy gives me the creeps, what was his name Jona...?"

" Jonathan Oswald" I intervened.

Joshua unlocks the car by moving the key clockwise in the driver's handle. Max jumps in the back and drops his jaw on his paws completely calm. To my surprise the dog seems normal now, I, even, tell Joshua same remark and he just nods in approval. I go to the other side, in the front passenger seat and meet his glazing blue eyes with a smile. The man next to me smiles back, we fasten our seatbelts and make a move back home.

The car slowly pulls out, making its way pass the parked vehicles. On the way down the hill, I notice the clock tower; we pass by a pub named after the alcohol 'Guinness' and then find our way to Great Malvern town center. The pubs on Belle

Venue terrace were suffocated with people drinking and smoking. I am not the type who liked visiting a pub in the heart of the day, but I prefer a " just me " space when possible. Joshua is quite the same. He avoids crowds and packed places. He feels more comfortable in a bit more intimate and lonely atmosphere.

Not long after we land in a car park outside Great Malvern, on the outskirts, somewhere by Poundbank. Joshua's parents were having a drink in the garden enjoying the touch of the sun. They greet us as we enter the back porch and Maxwell jumps on his owner, licking his cheek.

" How come you are a bit late? You went for a nice long walk?" questioned a blonde woman with sunglasses and very thin lips and quite predominant nose. She was wearing a blue sleeveless top with red shorts and garden slippers. She is

Joshua's mom, Martha. Next to her, is sat down, a slimmer gentleman with goat beard, bit double chinned and brown eyes. His hair is all combed backwards and black like raven's feathers. He is called Nathan. Nathan has always been closer to me than Martha. He has accepted me properly in the family than his wife. Even to this day I still feel there is like a glass wall between Martha and myself.

" How are you doing Denisa? Would you like a drink?"

" I am good, thanks. Just some juice or lemonade please!"

" Do you want me to make it or help yourself?"

" Yes I can do it. Thank you."

" So you two off today?! Anything interesting up the hills? Saw anyone up there ?" said Ethan watching me with a happy face. I just nod and make my way to the kitchen, the conversation melting behind me. Their voices become unclear.

The House On Black Hill

The cupboards were next to the fridge, but decided to have some decent juice instead of cheap squash. I am feeling like chills are going down my back and an easy breeze leaves its print on my neck making my body shiver . This sensation is not new to me, therefore I brush it off while I try to reach for the fridge handle. Inside it was quite empty : eggs, booze, cheese and some orange juice. I grab the box followed by pouring the orange liquid into a clean glass.

I return to the family but I pass by a shaving mirror hung up on the back door. Why the hell that was there I do not know. I stare at it finding it amusing and strange at the same time. I examine myself in the messy mirror. My hair is a mess, I try with my hand to tidy the bun, but something catches my eye. A black figure passes behind me with terrifying speed making me turning my head round. My heart is racing like mad and my eyes examine the stuffed kitchen in search of any presence..Nothing. I turn my whole body to watch more careful, but I cannot see anything out of the ordinary. Then, again, feel the breeze at the back of my neck but this time feels as someone is breathing. I get out to Joshua and his parents with the glass half trembling in my hand.

" Are you alright baby? You look pale?"

" Yes I am fine. Quite cool in the house. Thanks for the juice!"

" So anyone up the hills?"

"Well we met this old man that fallen down in some bushes and helped him."

" Oh gosh is he ok?" said Martha with superficial compassionate tone.

" Yes he is fine. Old man in his seventies. I helped him stand up. He asked us to come for a drink but we said no. He lives up the hills in a cottage deep in the woods. Just down Black hill."

" Had no idea there is even a house on there. Must be really old. Does he live alone?" asked Nathan.

" My god who can go up there to see him. Do you know him ?"

"Got no idea. Denisa remembers his name."

"I think he is Jonathan Oswald."

"Jeez what a posh name."

I indicate to Joshua that it would be time to return to our apartment to cook ourselves some food. He was hoping his mother would insist to stay for tea but the occasions were very rare. He grabs my hand waving bye to his parents and wishing a nice Sunday evening. We left the Range Rover and got into Joshua's black Ford Focus. His car was a lot cleaner and looked after. I tried to hold a conversation with Joshua based on what we'll have for supper. We decide on a takeaway. He will return to work tomorrow and so am I. Our discussion faded away as we approach the apartment car park. Joshua gets out of the car and embraces me briefly for a moment whispering in my ear:

"I know you got a bit uneasy with that old man. He looked funny to me too. But we won't go that way anymore."

My heart sank for an instant. A painful knot forms in my stomach. The memory of the figure in the mirror and the look of that cottage comes into my mind, flashing like scenes from a movie. It's sickly repeating, disturbing my mood. I curl my hands hiding my face in his chest.

"Ok. I love you."

" Love you too."

Chapter 3 – Followed by shadows

The next morning, Joshua left work really early being called to attend a severe problem. I was still half asleep when I felt a light kiss on the cheek and next thing the key turning into the yale. I wake up watching the spread cover of the bed and touching the side next to me: it is cold. The clock above the TV facing me indicates 7'o clock. I get up light-headed with a cold feeling invading my body. I have a morning freshen up, then dress into my navy blue uniform with buttons all over my chest. I skip breakfast as I am getting bit late and head downstairs to the car. Joshua had the company van, so the Ford was left at my discretion.

The House On Black Hill

As I get into the car, I try for one moment to pull myself together, forcing to put all the strange happenings from the previous day out of my mind. I drive to work at Brendon House, situated at the border of Great Malvern and Malvern Link.

Brendon House has been a nursing home since WWII and remains, until today, a place that always bring me chills; not just by the weird building structure, but by the hundred of souls that died unblessed and got lost within its walls. The nursing home didn't fit in any geometrical shape known : one side would be pointy, one side would be square, some would be circular. All of it painted in a sick, dirty white. The stairs that were raising from the circular lounge were old and weed was taking over it. That used to be the old fire exit.

I park the car at the front, lock it and then head towards the entry. Inside it was quite grandious, pretty straightforward : massive hallway all white again, on the right a beautiful staircase with cherry red carpet that takes you up. At the end of the corridor there were 2 big white double doors. That is where the kitchen is situated. I go through the hallway approaching the door pushing them slowly and greeting my two chefs: a young bloke and an old lady in her sixties. They were both dressed in white and concentrating on their preparations.

It was hard to read their expressions under the bonnets. The lad is Noah James and the lady - Rochelle Freya . Noah has always appeared slim as a plank, not too tall, not too short, with blonde hair cut in a 70s style and quite aged. His blue eyes were sunken in the head and cheeks seemed almost bony. The note of his chin would meet into a sharp form, intensifying his thinness.

Freya, on the other side, she was a plummy lady in her sixties with very short, red hair and thick lips, and same blue eyes as Noah. They were both nice to me. I, sometimes, would drag coming into work not knowing what to expect. My heart would go in my neck when I would see some floor colleagues doing their job wrong or sometimes upset me on purpose.

There were moments, when indeed, I refused to show up , but my rational side tortured me mentally. almost forcing me to head in this workplace. It was like a kick in the back from my conscience.

To my surprise, the washing up has disappeared. It wasn't a lot like other days, making my job enjoyable for the day. I just carry out my duties with pleasant attitude, jumping from one side of the kitchen to another. And that is how most of the day flies by. The sun outside got swallowed by the army of gray clouds. Not long after the dryness is covered in damp and start hearing thundering from far in the distance. A vague thunder. Freya leaves the shift not long after 3 o'clock and so does Noah before supper. I am left alone, in charge until 7 at night.

After carers would do their drink round, it becomes dead quiet. I start cleaning and cooking the supper. I notice at some point that some essentials have ran out so I have to pay a visit to the attic to stock up. That means I have to head upstairs.

A sentiment of uneasiness floods me as I despise attics. But I need stuff, so I must upstairs. I climb the beautiful steps examining the extravagant and elegant woodwork. I spend one moment admiring such a design. I always found this fascinating.

I pass the narrow hallway which is painted in yellow and red carpeted. It is quite. Deep silence. The brutal wind sometimes disturbs the peace by knocking in the windows or whispering aggressively. All residents' rooms are closed. Quiet. Too quiet! Not even one television on. There is a tensed atmosphere, quite different from ground floor's. My mind is blank. I feel bit of cold perspiration dropping down my spine which makes me shiver. I examine all closed doors : no names, just faded numbers.

Finally I reach the attic door. My breath is heavy and heart beats really slow. My whole body feels weak and heavy as I try to grab the door knob. I open it and stare at another set of steps. I raise my head trying to make what is one the top. I could not understand what was looking upon me or what. I flip the light switch and there is nobody. I go up the steps with ice touches going at the back of my neck. I can sense my hair standing. Nevertheless I grab what I need to head back down. The attic is damp, empty half lit. It is like a chamber stuffed with provisions and a bulb hung from the ceiling.

My legs were directing me back to the kitchen. I managed to get back on track with my bits and pieces and after I finished tea, I head to the car. Before getting in I could sense strongly someone's presence. I turn my head to see if there is any colleague coming out. No one. I look to the tree that is in front of the building. Its shadows are dancing in a evil manner in the struggle of the wind. But some of these shadows don't correspond to the shape of the willow tree. It is like someone is hiding behind it. I rub my eyes blaming the hard day. My mouth is dry. I decide in my head to go past the clock tower for a longer drive to clear my thoughts.

Joshua should be home before me. I drive off and carry on back home. I exit the car park, signal left and enter the main road. Everything is dull and damp. The sky is crying small drops on my windscreen making me contemplate its beauty. I try to brush off everything : the incidents from earlier, from yesterday. It feels like it haunts me, like it is following me. I could not forget the grudge that looked at us when we left the cottage on Black Hill. It has come with me since.

Joshua rings me and I pull over just after the clock tower to respond his call. The sky is darker than before …

"Hi baby I am home are you OK? Do you fancy some sausage and chips?'"

"Yes darling I am on my way back to you, Yes that sounds lovely' I answered in a low voice."

"Are you sure *you* are alright? You don't sound good."

" I am okay just had a really busy day and I am exhausted. I will see you in couple of minutes. Love you."

" Love ya too. Drive safely."

Something was stopping me from moving away. The rain finished its urge and now the water was flowing from all sides of the road down. I feel empty. Why? The reason is unknown. I stare at the wet windscreen. The trees behind the clock tower and waving to the wind. I can somehow make in the darkness of the shelter something standing there. A figure totally familiar with a horrid grin on his face supporting itself in a kind of stick. I try to make out what or who is it. Somebody heading up the hills to admire the view in the rain?!

No. It's not. It is Jonathan Oswald! But his face appears purple and full of scars and the grin shows the black hole because of lack of teeth. I turn my head back to the steering wheel, and with a unimaginable desperation to turn the car back on. My face is so cold that I almost feel my sweat turning to ice. My hands are white like untouched paper..

The car switched on with the first attempt and rushed back home. The wheels squeak violently as I pull out making the car sound almost furious.

When I returned to the apartment, Joshua greeted me with a puzzled look. He questions my behavior and my heavy perspiration. I looked to him as I fell into a lake.

I try to excuse myself and shower for several minutes while he sorts supper out. Before grabbing a chair, he hugs me from the back resting his chin on my right shoulder.

" What's wrong?" he asks in a warm voice.

Out of nowhere my vision blurs and hiccups are echoing in the kitchen. I try to wipe the salty pearls from the corner of my eyes. Bit clumsy, I manage to sit down and Joshua kneels before me. I just let it go.

" Am I fucking going crazy?? I saw a shadow at work in the attic, it felt like it followed me all the way to the car park and then when you rang me...I could swear I saw Jonathan Oswald in the woods. But he looked so sick, so blueish!"

" Denisa I have something to tell you. You are not losing your mind. Today I asked a mate at work that walks his dogs up there pretty often. I asked if he knew about that old man? He said he knew him briefly. But..."

" But...?"

" I don't know how to put this. I am shocked myself when he spoke with me...This Oswald is..is dead. He has been dead since 1990."

My eyes widen and my jaw almost drops.

" What do you mean dead? ' I nearly yell out. ' Dead?!!"

" I know ok? I know who that was. Could be someone

pretending to be him, but the description...It is impossible!'" says Joshua standing up. He places his hands at the back of his head trying to collect himself.

" Do you think we saw a ghost? In my culture we can see some spirits in solid shape. But it is said to show at night time, not daylight. And we never are meant to speak with them."

" I am not saying that but all this is shit! I touched that guy ... and felt solid... could have been a grudge, an apparition?"

" I felt really weird once we came closer to the house. It felt like it was watching us that there was someone by the window..."

" I don't know what would have happened if we entered that place!"

I suggest Joshua to say a prayer with me before our meal. He follows my instructions and repeats the words after me. The heaviness among us dissolves and it is replaced by peace. We carry on enjoying our supper and try to keep ourselves.. sane!

Chapter 4 – I can see you

Spent my afternoon reading what I discovered at the library about Jonathan Oswald. His photograph was there, his name was printed in the funeral section : April 1990. Exactly 23 years ago. My heart ponds each time I scroll over his picture and find the resemblance between then and now. According to the image I have in my head he hasn't age at all, except from I have seen him in the forest. On that occasion he looked dead to me, I mean recently deceased with blue-purple tone skin and more sunken eye than before.

I sit at the laptop desk, making notes about my research regarding the house on Black Hill. There was no mention about it in the Land Registry, no mention about any owner that would've built anything on that steep hill. Maybe there was never a cottage there? Maybe the grudge, the ghost created the mirage of a welcoming cottage to drag us into death?! I know from my faith and traditions that when a "spirit" calls for you, you must not answer, otherwise you will be cursed or even worse, die. This belief still lurks in our faith until today.

Joshua sensed something that day, whether it was mystic or just uneasiness, he felt it, and his intuition was right.

I support my chin with my palm trying to pull my thoughts together. A part of me wanted to go up the hills, in search for this house, to see if it is still standing; another part was cursing it and holding me tied up to the decision to stay put - to leave it behind. I feel drowned in a storm of sentiments. I always been sensitive to paranormal, but as I grew up I tried to deny and ignore this sensitivity.

Outside is daylight, just passed 4 o'clock. The birds are concerting various melodies that bring a sense of calmness and peace. I return to read a book I started a while ago: Schopenhauer's philosophy. I am in reach of something deep, for the meaning of life. Underneath my laptop, was laying one of Vladimir Nabokov's books. I turn the page shuffling through the story quite rapidly. Then, suddenly something catches my eyes in the small space of half open door. That leads to the hallway which was dark. Something is trying to disturb my lecturing.

An instantaneous movement crosses the petite gap. I could not make what it was, just feel the sensation as someone passes in a rush. My first instinct is to get up and check it.

Maybe Joshua arrived home and he believes I am napping. My body guides me automatically by the door , searching all directions of the corridor, and to my realization, it is bare. Satisfied with my investigation, I return to my seat reopening the book to continue the course of the story.

But... then I hear a slight noise, just like when Joshua taps the door to get my attention. There is no one. I stare with heaviness building over my shoulders and I feel my heart racing. The door is still half open. From the darkness of the hallway, from the opposite corner of the door, I can see something creeping, something sticking out with slow speed. It is black. Black hair. I shudder not knowing what is making itself known. It strikes completely in the small gap of the door like lightning on a stormy night.

A horrid figure of some kind, which resembles a woman

with matted hair, flowing down her face appears in front of me. Her face is ravaged, almost mutilated. Her bony, wrinckley cheeks reveal an evil grin, reflecting nothing but a toothless mouth, black as a hole. Her eyes shine with yellow strips matching those of a sick, dying person. Yet, it is just a head, not a body. It is only the upper part, sticking in the tiny gap left by the door. I scream in despair, can sense my blood reaching a boiling point. The chair falls behind me scared itself by the terrifying creature. I head and shut the door, using my own body as a shelter to stop anyone from entering the room. I begin praying loudly and loudly, sweat dropping down my face and neck. My hands are shaking on the knob. I want to open the door. A deep breath, afterwards a squeak sound...and grave silence. I run down the corridor to find nobody. I am beyond shock. I no longer feel safe, I grab my denim jacket, purse and keys from the hook and leave in most quickest manner. I am terrified...

* * *

Joshua finds me outside, on the streets in Malvern Link. The sun has gone long ago, the horizon dresses a gray coat and looks angry. My mind breaks the seconds of my encounter with that hideous figure. It is beyond my comprehension: who she was, what she was and what she wanted.

At the sight of my husband I couldn't resist but just run tearful into his arms, squeezing brutally his jacket. With my grip, I hide my face in his chest, I mumble my words, move my head strangely in hope to stop the tears. He cups my cheeks making my terror slide away for a moment. I can't find the words to explain what I have seen, don't find the bravery to return to our flat that now seems cursed. We establish to go for some supper at a restaurant. We manage to find an Indian nearby and stop to dine. I try to confess to Joshua what happened, but when he asks me about the ghost woman's description, I turn pale and words get stuck in my throat refusing to articulate. Instead, I show him my discovery made at the library regarding Jonathan Oswald.

Joshua was eating some of his curry still wearing his black uniform from work. He places his fork back on the plate and reaches for my mobile to see the photograph. He grabs the small device with the fingertips of both hands staring in astonishment. His eyes widen and the pink color from his cheeks dissolves into a shade of paleness. All the sudden his lips shrink and stick together.

" It can't be...it is impossible! He is dead! Damn dead!"

" I cannot believe it either. Who do you think that was in our flat?! I am scared Joshua!"

" We will go back to the flat and do something. I will check it."

" I will burn some incense and throw some water."

" Shall I tell my parents about it?"

" And what they can do?'"

I grab Joshua's hand as a consolation. Knowing that he will be there with me, is feeding me strength. We decide to return to our apartment after supper.

His work van was parked by Victory park. It was alone. Our journey to the vehicle is quiet. I notice on Joshua's face a sign of worry that he is trying to hide. Unfortunately his eyes done the mistake to be too sincere. Their shade of blue changed a bit. Pretty clumsy, he reaches for the key in his left pocket and presses a black switch making the car beep. I open the passenger door and the blonde man enters the driver's seat. After starting the engine, the vehicle moves forward freeing the parking space.

One of us interrupts the silence, making each other somehow tremble as our own words are icicles. We have to find out what is going on. Joshua intervenes, telling me about what one of his colleagues has been saying about Oswald and then suggests maybe we should return on Black Hill to bless it, to ask for somebody to help.

" They might think we are crazy. People don't believe in that anymore" I answered with a sour voice." Nobody will help us. Don't know what to do."

" Why don't we speak to a priest to do a cleansing or

blessing or I don't know some stuff like that."

Our conversation finishes with acid words. Joshua confesses what he has been experiencing, but it is not even close to what I have been through. I approve to try and get in touch with a priest or reverend.

The car moves slowly round some bends as we approach the flat. I can Joshua getting anxious and stressed. His hands tremble on the steering wheel and assisting to this scene does not bring me any comfort. I try to look in the hanging mirror searching for more cars following us but there are none. Instead, an uneasy feeling embraces me wildly. I look once more in the mirror as I am expecting someone to be sitting in the back. I can feel a presence. Joshua becomes more agitated. I can see the perspiration falling down his temple.

Once last glance as we prepare to stop. It was someone in

the back. I can feel it. I stare in the mirror and there he is. The dead looking man smirking at me – Jonathan Oswald. A strong yell made Joshua lose control over the steering wheel. He brakes excessively, the vehicle stopping in the end sideways. Both of us are in shock. The misty windscreen hides our petrified faces. Joshua raises his voice in despair:

" What the fuck was that??"

" I saw him baby. I saw Jonathan on the back seat, he was starring at me. I swear!"

" We could've had an accident! Shit!...SHIT! This is getting out of hand."

Joshua P.O.V.

Chapter 5 – Hidden terror

I try my best to function like a normal person at work, you know, I have bills to pay and a wife to look after; especially, after this trash that gets thrown at me in the last time. All this inexplicable shit is joggling with my brain causing me extra stress and headache. I could see depression slowly grabbing Denisa away from me, and I don't wanna lose that battle. I rescued her once don't wanna lose her and even myself over to *these* things...

The House On Black Hill

It's Monday morning and I get called into the manager's office. Damn! I need a coffee. I make a coffee first. Some demon inside me urges out; pushes me to a evil temptation : to borrow a cigarette from one of my work colleagues - but I do not wanna get dragged into more misery. My life is a mess at the moment : could have had a serious accident the other day. I cannot tell anyone, they will think I've gone fucking crazy...It's nuts! All this... I am 31 years god dammit! I wanna settle down. I make a black coffee and have a sip, snook in the maintenance storeroom. The room is suffocating, cluttered with tools and cleaning equipment. At the far back in the corner, there is a small improvised table with a folding chair. Next to it, is a kettle with a trivial sink.

One moment of silence … I drink every bit of it. However it doesn't last long, the peace disperses as somebody yells my name. I come out greeting one of my colleagues. His face is dirty from ash and paint covering the freckles. His hair is orange type color, and his gaze reminds me of the moss that grows on trees. Nice fella! From Ireland, I suppose, named Jamie.

He informs me that I am needed in the office.

" I know, I know" I respond as I wave as a "see you later". I leave as soon as I hear the squeak of the door. I head toward the end of the hallway and follow some narrow steps upstairs. All this reminds me of them towers from Disney cartoons where the princess is captive. All the paint has dimmed over the years, horrible peach-pink tone. Up the top, an open door greets me and in front of me with her big nose sunk in papers, was the manager. She can be difficult at times. Her appearance moves away from the concept of feminism:

plummy shape from many births, pale like a candle with dark hair arranged in a bun style. Her blue-green eyes are like smiling and shining in from the glorious light of the sun.

"Ah Joshua, I need you to do me a massive favor. A last minute one" she says blinking numerous times making me dizzy.

" What is it?"

" Darling, I need you to take some residents from Brendon house to picnic to the Quarry. Couldn't find a driver and I was told you can drive the minibus. Can you do that? I will pay you enhanced while you are out, but do not tell anybody! So what you say?"

" Fine. We got a deal, but today I have to leave a couple of minutes earlier. My wife needs me."

I return to my work after making arrangements for the

picnic. I knew how to get there. I will carry on with my duties once lunch is finished. I only have a couple of hours , next break will ring Denisa too. My morning flies by and all elderly people and carers were waiting for me in the minibus.

Our trip is quiet, all you can hear is the residents admiring the natural beauty of Malvern Hills, but I ignore their joy. For the first time I curse in my heart my hometown, this outstanding beauty marked my life, turned my marriage in hell and my mental state in a storm. I try to act normal at the surface, inside me, my essence crumbling like a ground slide.

The quarry is situated not far from Castlemorton. The ancient road that leads there remains covered in dust and dry grass all seasons. You would believe it is abandoned, but plenty of cars come here for visits, picnics and so on. I park close to the lake. It is like another world. All the sudden you are confronted with mountain stones where trees lay over, their beauty reflecting in the waves of the lake. The wind pats slowly over the surface of the water giving the illusion of movement. Everything else is still..and dead silence. Somewhere in the background I can hear fainted laughs and crumbled voices. I step forward guided by the mistique of the trees and the sound of the wind. I walk by the edge of the water ignoring my syncronised shadow from the surface.

I like it here, I inhale the spring scent. Something drags my gaze to the lake's margins. I look down following like a blurred trace, kind of a misterious fish swimming strangely..or could be a frog, even? I walk forward leaning gently to analyze the creature that now has stopped. It is floating and pinkish. It is not a fish or any aquatic creature that I have may known. The shape of it reveals a head, the size of a baby's but with sparkly tones. I grab a twig and poke it like a curious kid and to my realization: it is a doll's head...A mutilated doll's head lurking on the surface. For crying out loud! These kids nowadays are so irresponsable : trashing everywhere.

There is no way I can get hold of it and discard it. The water is deep. I carry on walking examining the phone screen. A photo of Denisa and I , makes me chuckle. Crap! Forgot to ring her. No signal. Just my luck! I am farther now, no voices can be heard, no human sounds. Still, can hear shuffling behind me. I turn my head towards the woods. The mixture of shadows and lights gave the perfect contrast of painful vision.

But beyond that palette of blended lights-shadows game, I can distinct clearly one misty figure standing. A figure of a woman. Her face is ravaged, I cannot make out any expression of her glance , if I can call it so. The outfit is so unclear. In my anticipation, a shape of a dress, maybe black, or very dark gray, hangs over her body. She makes my heart race. I can smell death from her; a rotten scent and flavor of decay. That is it! Corpse smell ! *Death...* Again *death!*

I raise my hands and place them behind my head as a desperation gesture. Shit ! Not here too! It just can't be ! It is following me?!

I run back to the minibus slamming the door and turning the radio off. I notice a blessed talisman off Denisa. I grab it trying to find a source of comfort in it. I squash it in my fist, my shoulders burning from unseen weight; which then disappears suddenly when my mobile vibrates in my right pocket. I take it out shocked by the image of this weird message from an unknown number :

"The grudge is not in the house...The house is the grudge!..."

My lips rub against each other like mad. I try to take a screenshot and ring Denisa. The mobile makes connection but no answer.

"Come on pick up. Come on! Fuck ! Please pick up!" I try to redial her number but again no answer from other end. My nerves are over the top, my blood races through my veins, making my cheeks flush. I wanna drive home and bang at that fucking door, tell her off and hug her. But work is in my way.

In several minutes everyone is in and I drive them back. Everybody is grateful and thank me for the ride. I try to force a smile but I get into my work van and rush back home. My mind is flooded with denial and doubthfulness. I race my way back to the flat praying everything to be fine. It *will* be fine!

Gotta be!!

With rapid moves I lock my van and head brutally up the stairs, my footsteps echoing in the whole building. It feels so empty. Once I reach the door, I grab the handle, my hand freezing for an instant. That very instant I sense a familiar scent and it is not death, it is homemade meal. Made my presence known in the apartment screaming Denisa's name. There is no sign of her. Then, she appears from the shower with the towel wrapped around her body, her hair still dripping. I just grab her wildly by her waist pinning her against the bathroom door.

" Joshua what are you doing?"

Her brown eyes show signs of fear and mine a relief mixed with possession. Didn't get the chance to reply properly, my lips crushed on her forming a gentle kiss. It evaporated like my fears from earlier.

"Why you didn't bloody answer me?? I was worried sick!!"

"I was having a bath, long soak. I really needed it. Tea is ready and..I really need to talk to you!"

" So do I."

I had a freshen up, putting my joggers on with a red T-shirt. My wife puts some lounge wear on. We are sitting next to each other and eating our supper : sausage and beans casserole with homemade bread. The house was covered in that delicious flavor. Bored of the soaps, I turn the TV off. Don't really know how to start this conversation, don't wanna scare her more than she is. I know she had my mother coming over, just for the sake of company. After last encounter she didn't like being alone in here. Although she preferred solitude, but this time is was fear in the way.

" Today I saw something..or someone by the quarry. It looked just like that woman you told me..she looked dead! Like rotting..and even the smell.. And then..." my hand begins shaking, making me stop talking.

" And then?..."

I reach out for my phone to show her the screenshot, but..it is gone. I explore the menu for good few minutes and no sign of it. What the fuck??

My explanation comes out fragmented as my own voice is shuddering. It is beyond my understanding. Denisa grabs my hand as she sees me alarmed. " What the message say?" I hear..

" Something something the grudge is not a house..the house is the grudge. The last bit I remember exactly!"

" I tried to get in touch with a priest...So far all it can be done is a cleansing."

My face brightens up.

" And ..that is good news right?"

" From my belief, a cleansing is not enough. I do try to believe it is our desired answer!..."

Chapter 6 - Pale hope

I can read the distress in Denisa's eyes. My heart shrinks in pain every time this happens. It hurts a lot more now than before; can't even put it in words.

She gets up from her seat holding the half full plate with food. A wall of silence builds up between us and it feels thick as a glass barrier. I can't comfort her ; don't have that power anymore. All this shit has consumed me.

Putting the dish in the sink, Denisa stares at the tap, just standing so immobile as a mannequin. I can hear rare and vague drops nudging, echoing in the kitchen. It is *her* !*She* is crying! As I get up, I sense the silence melting away. I grab her by the shoulders making her turn around, so that, she faces me. She hides her face in my red T-shirt. It is all that fucking house to blame! *That house and that man...*

Later on she manages to fall asleep in my arms, TV running smoothly in the background. A chair is pinned against the door, securely keeping it locked; all this just to brush our fear and replace it with a drop of safety. Our bedroom is the only space where we feel secure. This entire curtain of despair is pushing us down the madness path. It's strangulating us. Could it be really, the house on Black Hill?

I never believed in ghosts. All of it was bullcrap to me, but for Denisa it is a cultural thing. I don't know, but I manage to dose off for the rest of the noon. My grip on Denisa loosens, giving her the freedom to move under the blanket. The sun is still up. Around 6 o'clock, I rub my eyes to clarify my vision as a familiar tone woke me up and the one to blame was the phone which beeped. An email or SMS? From whom?

I sneak my hand getting hold of her mobile. We never hide secrets from each other. A message from a person named Reverend Mathias. Finally, some good news. I try to build a smile after muting the phone and abandoning it on the bedside cabinet. Selfishness stabs me for now, I don't wanna be bothered. I wanna hold Denisa and enjoy this minute of calmness. She can read it later.

I don't know how the rest of the afternoon flown away. I kept starring at the ceiling for the past couple of hours that I lost count. Everything surrounding me is just quietness...too much...it is like swallowing us..The sound of my breath and heart touch the silence like a hand on a glass and then torn it same as broken paper. All this stillness causes me cramps in the my stomach, aching pain that is similar to sickness. And then, a gesture brings me back to my senses. A warm gesture and legs moving across the duvet make me aware. Denisa is waking up. That bit of nap made her face lighten up, all the sadness and worry have erased magically in her sleep. A gentle touch forming a soft kiss on the forehead made her raise her chin, her gaze meeting mine. We decide to have a late hot drink, some milky coffee. Denisa grabs the phone from the bedside cabinet scrolling through notifications. Her voice reaches out to me in a high pitch:

" The priest came back to us. He said we can drop in anytime to see him. He is available. Joshua let's go!"

" Hold on a minute, I need to get dressed. And where are we going?"

" We need to go to Malvern Wells and see this priest at once Joshua. He is at St. Christopher's church."

I remain stiff for a moment trying to figure out the name of that church. It's name is invading my head scratching my ears. It's as somebody keeps repeating it again and again insanely.

The word itself "church" stabs me, scratches me hideously. I cover my ears but the sound goes beyond my flesh. I resist somehow thinking how important this is for *Denisa,* for *us*, for *me*....

In between Denisa manages to freshen up. The black jeans put a sophisticated print on her, although the cartoon T-shirt was ruining the outfit, making it an almagam of tastes.. I wear just normal joggers and changed my shirt with a light grey one.

Something inside me makes me grab her hand bit brutally,

her puzzled look questioning my sudden behavior.

" We need to go! NOW!"

She follows me like an obeying child, my gestures probably triggering back that sadness, that roughness of the situation. It was too difficult to explain it what might've happened at the house if we stayed there longer. I wanted to hurt her, but it was not my desire, it was like a dictated instruction.

Once we get into the Ford, I feel free, released by the mysterious anger.

" I'm sorry Denisa. I'm sorry baby, I had to take you out as soon as possible. I felt like something was taking over me, that if...we didn't leave..I might have done something bad!But...it is not me!"

Her glance shakes of fear mixed with care. Don't look at

me like that! That ghost is manipulating my feelings. Does it try to turn me against you?!

With the key turning in the ignition, the engine begins to rawl as we pull out on the main road. Nature is pouring it's beauty across the narrow roads. The concrete lanes are disguised in the abundance of vegetation. It is quiet again! The lane swirls like a snake, the leftover trail of death being sensed after every sharp bend. At the far end, the sharp tower of the church dares to touch the sky, the steel tiles glowing powerfully just like God Himself sits on top as a witness of the world. It is a small building, the tower showing a separate glory as a separate *entity*. We abandon the car at the front and head to the main entrance. This splendid wooden door was carved in two, giving the impression of a far forgotten time. We thought for a moment we were stuck in the past century.

A metallic ring was attached to the door. Denisa steps forward knocking so loudly that you could hear it repeating inside the building. A figure sneaks out greeting us. His appearance inspires me kindness, a feeling that I almost forgot about. His eyes show a different shade of blue and the bags from underneath tell me his age somehow - late sixties. His head had a sharp chin and his outfit was typical of a priest's : black hanging down like a robe. It is getting dark he can make just about our presence.

"May I help?"

" Father Mathias? I am Denisa Sanders and this is my husband, Joshua. I have messaged you a while ago about a meeting and maybe a confession.."

" Oh yes, bit late though..."

Denisa steps in with a pleading voice almost begging.

" Please Father, it is urgent!"

Seeing the wave of tears building up in her eyes, Mathias opens the door wider and invits us in with a sweet tone waving his hand. We are guided after the chapel where he had arranged a table with cups, tea pot and different religious books pilled up. Then his figure disappeares behind a velvet curtain. The painted glass is now dark, sign that outside the night is taking over. I grab Denisa's hand as a consolation until we sense the figure of reverend approaching.

He returns with a tray with beautiful cups of tea and places it carefully in front of us. Lifting one of the cups, he sips from his drink rubbing his lips to remove any excess of it. His eyes wait for us to start the purpose of our visit. Denisa with a trembling voice, tells our atrocities. The reverend watches her posing as a good listener, massaging his chin from time to time, making me wonder if he believes our story.

Mathias arranges superficially his collar. He sighs nodding his head in both directions.

" My child, I am afraid this is beyond my power! I can come and do a deep cleansing, but I cannot do more than that!"

We agree for him to carry out the purifying ceremony the next day as we will be off together. Our discussion dreads as we don't get the answer to our problems. The priest accompanies us to the door. Denisa's walking is numb and clumsy, I can see the her thoughts are somewhere else.

" I suggest you find a medium . I have heard of one lady called Laura Martnen. She is very gifted. Um..she used to come to me quite often..She lives on the outskirts on Bishop's Lane. Go ask there and mention me."

The House On Black Hill

A medium? You kidding me? First churches, now this...

*　*　*

We return home and I just want to pack some things to get out. For the first time I just feel like I want to give up. No! This is not *me* ! *I* don't give up !

I analyze my reflection in the mirror, something is not right, I look myself, yet I feel like someone else is dictating my thoughts, my moves and my feelings. Lately, my pure care and love fades into a hole of pain, despair, sometimes hatred. Somehow, a wave of calmness comes over me, my head feels clear and relaxed, like after a storm.

Chapter 7 A drop of truth

" *You are so close and, still, feel so far from me. Your body is here, but your presence is not.*" The emptiness of the room strangulates me. Having her here does not bring any relief. Our marriage hangs by a thread. I am trying to function as a normal person at work, I try to support Denisa, but I am falling apart.

Last night both of us fell asleep with cold hearts, separate; each one of us, on their own side of the bed, not daring to touch each other. After breakfast we argued, the stillness of the room got disrupted by the wave of voices, rain of heavy words and the sound of slamming mug on the table.

My eyes fall on her, quietly watching her, but she ignores my gaze.

" I'm...I'm sorry for earlier" I try to approach her, but then her silhouette raises and half-turns, moving across the hallway. Her footsteps echo, intensifying the emptiness of the apartment. Feels to heavy in here. I try to follow her, but she does not seem to pay attention to my presence. I only creep half way by the door step. She treats me with ignorance. Yes, this ignorance sends me icicles down my back. I feel by body shuddering. Denisa opens the wardrobe and with fast gestures, takes out just her belongigs. With an unfamiliar quick pace, she throws them all across the bed. A force tells me to intervene, it palpitates on my conscience.

I step in front of her stopping her from reaching the wardrobe. She tries to brush past, but my blood pumps hot in my veins. My patience is at the limit. My head is about to explode with anger.

I reach for Denisa's wrists and wave them abruptly breaking the heaviness of the atmosphere. She sees I am mad. Her eyes are glowing; shiny drops building rapidly trying to escape down the cheeks. The chocolate shade of her look has faded or maybe I haven't seen it carefully for a long time.

" Don't *you* touch me! I am leaving!! I had enough ..of this..of *you.*" *I can't take it anymore. If I carry on like this I will die...*

" Denisa, you are not going anywhere! Stop acting like this!"

" I had enough Joshua! I feel like I am going to die. Like we are going to die! We are not the same. *You* changed. That's why I go back to Romania! I had enough!...I am scared..I am alone..."

My heart sinks. My whole world crumbles before my eyes. Her last words penetrate my ears and burn them. I feel like I am on fire. She packs some bags while I just stand starring at nothing. The shock is too big, my legs start to weaken. I realize in the end that this is reality. The zipper's sound brings me back like awakening from a dream. My arms surround her, stopping her from moving. She obeys my gesture and responds back to my embrace. Denisa's back pushes into my chest as I tighten the grip in the attempt to make her quit from escaping. Her warm hands against mine burns all the coldness that nested between us.

" Please don't go! I love ya! I want you to stay!...Please"

" I...am ...scared Joshua...but I love you too."

Finally, the sobbing sounds and hiccups can he heard in the

room. Cold and salty drops melt on my burning hands. Some of them evaporate, some land on the floor. I support my chin on her shoulder :

" It will be okay, we will find a solution for this..."

Denisa escapes my grip and her face turns so that it meets mine. Raising my right palm, I wipe away the remaining tears. We never argued like this..We never confronted each in such a manner so we start hating each other. It is like the ghost is dictating our feelings and our souls. It is trying to break us apart. She gulps while reaching for my hands and guiding me to the dining room. There, I am shown my seat, Denisa pulling hers closer, meditating carefully perhaps on her words, how to start the discussion without triggering a confruntation. The wind outside amplifies in power scratching our balcony doors, producing a agonizing squeak.

" Can we please contact Mrs Martnen? I know how skeptic you are about this stuff, but Joshua please we have not other option. We gotta try this, otherwise I feel like I will lose my mind!"

I tilt my head proving my defence followed by a deep sigh. In the end, I agree and give Denisa my permission to get in touch with this lady. A painful smile rises in one corner of her lips, a small smile that hides both hope and sadness . I try to build a smile too, but don't have the energy for it.

Denisa holds the mobile, with her right hand going across the screen in up-down motions, then typing with both her thumbs. Slowly she brings the phone closer to her left ear clearly hearing a long beep, sign that is ringing. A slim fainted voice answers and Denisa speaks with her on a professional tone, willing to arrange an appointment. I just sit nervous playing with my fingers, my wife reading my anxiety on my face. Her eyes lighten up, her words shake with some kind of excitement. After her telephonic conversation ends, Denisa releases it on the table and holds me in a tight hug. We have to get ready for the appointment that will take place the next day, but I have to work. So work comes in our way. The manager owed me a favor, perhaps she will be able to help me. I have to contact her and make an excuse. I make the phone call and the voice that greets me is lovely and snobby as usual. As soon as I mention the possibility of not showing up for work tomorrow, her tone changes drastically. I face some telling off like this shit is not a kind of emergency.

" Listen, family is more important. This is very unexpected. A death in the family, you have to be understandable."

" Ok ok...I see..How long you will be off for darling?"

" Just 2 days, I will sort everything, please!"

" Very well then..not a problem!"

" Thanks"

" That manager of yours is such an awful woman!" intrerupts Denisa.

" She can be a pain, but she is alright with me. Let's get ready."

* * *

We find ourselves in front of this big, white house, in a rectangular shape with half circle driveway. The walls show cracks here and there, it is stuffed with creamy colored windows, six all together. The roof has been refitted, denoting a touch of new with slight extravagant note. Outside, the golden circle is way gone; an explosion of colors battle on the horizon separating the end of a day from invasion of the night. Denisa approaches the main entrance hesitantly, her glance examining the mansion in detail. We are facing a navy blue sculptured door, pretty modern, not plain, not too exagerated. Again, this gives the impression of new, of living. All mansion's roof together with the door fight for the balance of contrast : new elements against old shabby windows and tatty aesthetical marks. Her knuckles bang repetitively against the wood , producing a sound of fullness as if you would hit a trunk with a stick. The door opens slightly and a figure sneaks from behind, meeting us with a charming look. The dress covered with pink floral prints, dance in the wind , patting her knees gently. A few locks of red hair fall over her round cheeks seeking freedom from the tight bun. My attention is caught by the blood red lipstick this lady is wearing, revealing her extremely thin lips which lost their youth spell. She watches us with astonishment and introduces herself with a pleasant, low pitch voice :

" Hi there... How can I help? " says the lady as she opens the door wider.

" Good afternoon, we have an appointment with Laura Martnen.. My name is Denisa Sanders and this is my husband, Joshua."

The woman stretches her hand ,slowly leaning forward expecting a shake, giving her the opportunity to introduce herself. Denisa does the honors, but for a moment I am lost, I don't hear their voices anymore, just see their lips moving. My own name penetrates my ears making me aware again of my surroundings. I follow Denisa into the house. We walk down the corridor flooded with semi-darkness. Everything is painted in a type of orange, a sickening color that brings me back odd memories from hospital and nursing homes.

At the far end of the corridor, few translucent strips of light fall on the door mixing with the shade of the woodwork. Laura Martnen steps ahead and opens the door, complaining about the heated knob. Denisa stands by my side watching the so called reception room. The immense rug has a faded pattern, that erased with time and lost its beauty from so many people who stepped on it. In the center, there is a brown leather couch, big enough to host two people. A small coffee table in a oval form, adds elegance to the room; across from it two velvet brown chairs complete the extravagant touch.

From the ceiling hangs this ancient type chandelier with dusty crystals. The light is very poor, but mystical. Laura sits in one of the velvet chairs offering to make a coffee. We really need to get to the point.

Her gaze changes, her eyes shining with golden brown sparkles. She turns serious remaining silent for brief seconds, giving her chance to cross her legs.

She moves her head watching, almost starring at Denisa, then her eyes fall on me. Still, she doesn't insist as much, and returns her look at my wife. The atmosphere gets tense, my heart is hammering without any reason. My legs play madly on the rug. It doesn't feel right!

" You haven't come to see me for counseling, have you? It is something else bothering you!"

My words freeze in my throat, my lips tremble and icy touches seem to make my body shiver with fear. Who is this woman? Denisa remains stiff, quiet not knowing what to answer.

" Mrs Martnen, we were sent here by Reverend Mathias." I interfere almost yelling. Laura's face turns friendly, but keeps the professional look when she hears the Reverend's name.

" Ah, I see...I knew there was something unusual. How is Mathias, bless him? Anyhow, what brings you here?"

" Our house is haunted...our life is haunted...We went for a walk on Black Hill a couple of weeks ago and met this old man. Joshua helped him and he invited us to his cottage,but it looked abandoned for years. Later we started experiencing terrifying things...I saw this..this face of a woman. Joshua says he feels like he wants to hurt me, we argue a lot...We feel watched all the time in our flat."

" I understand and have you tried to do a cleansing?"

" The Reverend sent us to you. I am scared. I feel like I am losing my mind!"

I keep messing around with my fingers, gathering them to form a fist and then without realizing I hit the arm of the couch violently.

" This man is dead! We looked for some information about him and he is damn dead!!! And yet I saw him in my car, Denisa saw him by the clock tower! It is something going on!"

" Joshua please! I understand you are frustrated!"

"Then will you please help us find a solution! Everywhere we go , we face closed doors! You are our only hope."

" From what you are saying this is not a man, this sounds like a demonic entity that just took the appearance of this man. You, Denisa have a special sensitivity like a medium, hence why you saw the woman. You saw it's true form. By the sounds of it, it is using Joshua to get to you. It tries to ruin you."

" Then...what do you suggest?"

"I say to pay a visit to your apartment if you allow me and see what I can sense, then I want you to show me this House on Black Hill. I want to go there and see what I can find. We will take it from there."

" What about you come with us right now please?! I am not going back to the flat knowing a demon or whatever lurks there..." I say acidly. My voice sounds sour, I can feel it disturbs Denisa as she fixates me with her chocolate eyes.

Laura nods in approval, then stands up waiting for us to follow her. Being guided by her, we make our way out and head back to the car. I open the door abruptly and enter the vehicle, starring for an instant in the rear mirror. Laura is getting in her car, a dark red Nissan, pretty newish. Once I see she is ready to go, I start the engine, put in gear and accelerate with the desire and excitement that we might have found a solution that all this nightmare...

Chapter 8 – Behind you...

"What is this woman doing in our flat??"

I get this voice invading my head, strongly demanding what is Laura doing in our apartment. I know it is not my inner voice; I know it is this *thing!*

Denisa serves Mrs. Martnen a cup of coffee and sit down at the dining room table while I retreat in the bedroom, trying to calm down my inside urge for pain. I know is not me, I can feel it!

Minutes later I sense Laura's presence coming to our bedroom, finding me sitting on the edge of the bed. She fixates me with her gaze like a vultur. Something in me is about to explode. A knot is born in my chest expanding in my ribcage.

The House On Black Hill

* * *

I find myself pinned against the wall, with my head lowered so that I face the ground. The floor is dirty; a gray carpet of dust lies like untouched snow. I don't know when my mother cleaned the kitchen last time. I take a few steps towards the back door, raising my head to examine my own reflection in the smudgy mirror.

I cannot believe how coward I am. How easy I have abandoned Denisa and left her with that odd woman, Laura. My mother calls me but I ignore her voice. She, eventually, returns from downstairs to check on me. Her outfit if I can call it so, is typical for a summer day: a gray vest not very feminine, and blue shorts, plain as paper. Her hair denotes untidiness as well : a messy bun where curls keep escaping.

The worry that fills her blue eyes, it's something I haven't seen in years. With a wide look , she examines my face commenting about the paleness of my skin.

" You look rather sick, almost dead!"

Sick yes...dead?! Maybe, not yet!

" Joshua what happened to you? You look so unwell! Come and sit down! I will make you something to eat."

Her maternal touch melts my heart. She hasn't been like this for a very long time. Mom places her hand on my shoulder guiding me to the leather couch. It is tatty, yet comfortable. Silence invades the living room, but proves to be a blessing. No terror, no anger,no madness!

Within minutes, she returns with some french toast, my favorite when I was a kid. The plate lands gently on the coffee table next to me, then mother sits in another seat; her blue gaze starring at me – begging me to start eating. Obeying her indirect command, I tuck in; crunching noises taking over the quietness of the room.

" Why don't you tell me what is wrong ? What is going on between you and Denisa?"

" You won't believe me..."

" Darling, I believe you after all. Now, what has that girl been doing to you?...She is not cheating on you, is she?"

" No mom! No!" I feel anger running through me. That is the last thing I want to hear this moment. " She is good to me! It is something else...Our apartment is..um..it's fucking HAUNTED!"

Her eyes widen and sparkle with surprise. I can read the notes of skepticism in them just like an opened book. She probably questions my sanity at this point; if I am doing something out of the ordinary. She might be thinking that I take drugs, all that crap. I surely, don't!

" Did you say your flat is haunted?! Are you sure? What makes you think so?!"

" Mom, I saw a woman in there, then she vanished..um..we had things moving around and I..I feel exhausted all the time. I have this urge to hurt...to kill.."

And then, I meet the frozen glance of someone I don't recognize. My mother's caring expression disperses and I am confronting myself with the look of a petrified woman. Shocked, she continues to stare at me, not daring to articulate a word.

" We got something in that flat mother!It all started that afternoon when we took Maxwell for a walk up the hills and...and met that man. And that man is dead!"

" Maybe you need to see a vicar Joshua."

" I've already been and it's no use."

Slamming the plate on the petite table, I get up and head back into the kitchen. My phone was on the counter. All of the sudden I remember to text Denisa. I grab the mobile and brighten the screen by pressing an aside button. While texting her I feel guiltiness building up inside me. How could I be so selfish and weak?...

Denisa's P.O.V.

Chapter 9 : Back to where it began

I receive a text message from Joshua. My phone beeps in my pocket, but I don't bother reading it. He has abandoned me!

Laura and I climb the steep hill through the thick vegetation. All grass swallows us; it feels as if arms are trying to reach for us and grab us in their clutches. The path itself camuflages under the carpet of moss. We step over damp rocks; at the same time,swinging our arms in both directions, in attempt to remove the bushes which lean before us, blocking our view.

The journey seems never-ending and I am tired. My heart pounds like a hammer. My inner voice curses Joshua. I want to scream; the knot of doubtfulness nests within me and it grows causing me pain. I just wish that night I escaped his grip, grabbed my stuff and left – but – he had to stop me.

Do I still love him? I do.

Have I started to hate him? It is a seed of hatred planted.

Laura guides me to the top of the hill : The Black Hill. This is where it all began. But, we reached Black Hill by a different route. The overlook is breathtaking, the picture is so peaceful. It is a peace I haven't felt in weeks. My body relaxes under the touch of summer breeze. I forgot June has already arrived .

I only want to sit here and inhale the scent of peace, enjoy the gentle move of cooling wind. Laura points to the Beacon, she breaths heavily as she supports herself against a tree. Then, she sits on a nearby bench.

" Oh dear, this is too much for me. What a trip, but it was worth it. Where is this house?"

I point with my right hand :

" Behind those bent trees."

" We will go there in a bit . The Beacon is just ahead."

A snake-like path leads us to the army of trees. Laura steps back and I get in front showing her the way to the house. The summer sun shines same as that day : blinding us. The sooner we reach the trees, the better will be. All splendid sunlight disappears as we enter the little forest. Shadows and chilliness combine into an eerie mixture. Even, the wind sounds unpleasant and cold. It fights us striking with chilly spikes ; I am freezing as I am standing in the middle of a winter day. Something pushes me to text Joshua and tell him about my decision and the fact that we are on Black Hill. I sneak the phone back in the pocket followed by a beep sound. Laura doesn't seem affected by the cold atmosphere. Everything feels so heavy..so dense. These trees hide the truth from us. The red haired lady examines the surroundings sinking in a deep concentration.. It is like she is in a sort of a trance.

Then, my hair stands up and my flesh curls at the sight of the house. Exactly same creepy windows and scruffy door. This time we haven't seen it, a few chains of weeds took over the walls of the building. Except for that, the house remained the same.

" It's here. Am I right?" Laura's voice deepens, sounding stronger and almost demanding.

I know deep down that is not her speaking, it is the house or whatever inhabits it.

" Yes-yes."

She turns her head to face me and her gaze becomes cold and rigid.

" Jonathan is in there."

My eyes trace the whole house stopping at the windows that stare back at me with hate , absolute pure evil. And they are approaching us...closer and closer..

What have I done? With the corner of my eye I can make out what Laura's moves are. She focuses on the house again, but more precisely on the upper windows.

" This man is not Jonathan Oswald. Jonathan was killed. He died here, but you see it is not him you see. It is the demonic presence of Black Hill."

"What do you mean?..."

"This entity used this man's appearance to deceive people and drag them into their own death. So many souls are trapped on this land : some are stuck, some seek revenge."

She digs in one of her pockets, grabs a lighter and a bunch of dried herbs. She burns some of it and begins to wave it in circles hoping to cleanse the area. With circular moves Laura recites an incantation that is in a language I have never heard before. As she carries on with her ritual, a shadow raises in the left window, slowly shaping into a being similar to a woman. Her body remains vague , appears to wear a dark,long dress; but I can see clearly her upper side: a head with black, knotted hair which covers half of her face. One distinct feature terrifies me: the large mouth that reveals its razor sharp teeth.

My feet weaken, the ground trembles beneath my feet. That evil smile I picture it in my head. It invades my mind and its evil laughter scratches my ears...

Chapter 10 - I am coming after you..

My vision turns misty; I cannot make out what I see, don't know where Laura is. The ground's coldness touches - my fingers, turning them numb and pale. My legs are also stiff. It is as if a spell holds be bond down. Seeing that entity, hearing it laughing make me believe it might be the face of death itself. And - I am approaching it.

The ground's coldness stabs my body. Pain won't leave my fingers, this cold beast bits every part of me, making me shiver and afraid. I do not dare to move.

Somewhere, in the distance Laura's voice repeats like a church bell. I don't figure out her words, but I recognize her voice. The demonic force pushed me on the ground with an invisible strength. I begin to wonder if I am still alive...

One cold tear peers out from the corner of my left eye and slides down the cheek, rapidly melting into the dry, chilled grass. The sky is missing; it is covered by the abundance of leaves and branches.

Then, a silhouette leans down on me obstructing my view. It is unclear – this doesn't scare me anymore. I force myself to close my eyes, but a violent shake brings me to my senses. My upper body shakes under a brutal grip and my vision is now crystal-clear.

"No! No! No! Wake up Denisa, please! You have to stay with me!"

Joshua? Could this be a dream? No! It is indeed him; he came to rescue me, but I thought he has abandoned me.

Shocked, I stare into his topaz eyes; not knowing what my

next move will be.

I try to raise my hands and wrap them around his neck.

"Thank goodness you are safe! We need to get out of here!"

Laura was exhausted. She was resting by a nearby tree trunk, praying for my salvation. After, I pulled myself together, she indicates for us to get away from Black Hill as soon as possible. Joshua helps me stand up. My pain in my ankle builds up; perhaps one of them twisted in the fall.

My husband decides it is best to carry me until we reach Saint Ann's well. I notice how light I became. All the stress, the long working days and sleepless nights have been taking a toe on me.

Silence raises between Joshua and I. Laura offers us indications and leads the way. The single sounds I hear distinctly are crumbled leaves, rattling under their feet. My eyes concentrate on the sky : peaceful and again patched with clouds. Temperature returns pleasant and warm again.

* * *

A brick building stands before us. The quietness flows around us as we arrive. Maybe, we are the only living beings around this place. Upstairs, a plain balcony remains a perfect spot to sit and enjoy the view. Joshua manages to get me sat down and catch his breath after all that trip. Between gasps for air, Laura arranges her hair and drinks her water quite noisy. Both of them look so serious; which worries me. As I sit with guiltiness invading me, those two were under the balcony discussing what has been happening. Between words, I try to remain focused, but I get lost in my own storm of thoughts. I have reached my limit! I can't, any longer, hold my tears : my anxiety, my inner pain.

The empty walls echo with hiccups and gulps. How foolish this is! Despair is slowly showing its teeth, making me lash out even more. I gather my fists and hit madly on my legs. Shit!

Joshua returns to check on me and grabs my wrists, watching me worried and upset at the same time.

"What the hell are you doing?Stop it!"

"Just leave me alone..please. You shouldn't be here anyhow!"

"Are you crazy? I am your husband and I love you, you silly!"

He stops my protests by releasing my hands, then wraps his arms around me, resting his head on my shoulder.

" I love you, I really do. I don't want to lose you to this thing.

I want to protect you, not hurt you!"

" But I don't want to feel lonely and painful. If you are not with me, I am alone and vulnerable... I have no one."

" You got me, ok? Me leaving was the stupidest thing I have done."

We both sense Laura's presence coming up the steps. She wishes to carry out a discussion regarding our options.

" I am sorry to say that I don't know how effective my cleansing will be"

"Then what do you suggest?"

" I need some time to dig deeper into this matter. Joshua, in the meantime, you must take Denisa away from that apartment. None of you is safe there. Once, I find a way to sort this out, I will be in touch. We are dealing with an evil entity which has thrist for death."

The House On Black Hill

" I understand."

Joshua returns his face towards me; my figure reflecting into his blue eyes.

" I know you are not gonna like this but we need to go and stay with my parents. I will have to go to work and get some leave booked as soon as possible."

" I am going to lose my job at this rate, if I don't go back."

" Denisa your well-being is more important than a fucking job. I need to look after you. I cannot do same mistake twice. I will not run away again..Will you be able to walk?"

" I think so..."

At the bottom of the hill, the silence lurks all around. The car park seems empty as well. Few birds throw a vague concert, and a pleasant dusk scent dances in the air : the smell of summer.

The House On Black Hill

Once again, I thank Laura as she returns home anxious after a battle with the unseen; and we head back to Joshua's parents.

Before our arrival , we try to announce our stay and treat them to a takeout. I know Nathan will be supportive, but not sure about Martha response with me being around her.

Joshua stops the car in Barnad's Green. He kisses me on the forehead and heads to a chippy. Not far away from the roundabout, there it is : my workplace. A few coworkers walk past our car, not remarking me. I try my best to avoid being seen. I overhear some commenting about myself. All of them walk in line like ants. Waiting for Joshua's return seems endless, although the sun is hiding and the curtain of darkness settles in. He comes to the vehicle carrying a paper-bag which steams. Before getting in, he offers it to me to hold it till we reach his family's house. It is evening and I getting tired...

Once parked the car, Joshua and I get into the house somehow hesitant. Nathan greets me in his brown gown and takes me to Joshua's old room.

"Make yourself at home,dear! Bless, I hope you feel better soon." says Nathan grabbing me in a hug and giving me the chance to inhale his fresh aftershave smell.

" We both care for you, Martha and me"

His remark makes me smile. He tries his best to comfort me despite the situation.

The House On Black Hill

Chapter 11 : Another route

The outside weather is hostile today. I managed to send an absence form to my work, trying to justify the reasons for my disease. Of course, my manager probably raised her eyebrows in doubt when she received my doctor's note through someone else. My job is in the game, but I don't care about that anymore: - I just want my life back. Slowly, I am grabbed by the claws of despair.

Some days, I don't make out the dates or the time any longer. I got stuck in this mist of nothingness. I feel I belong nowhere.

As I sit at the scratched and uncovered desk, I glance at the hanging clock. A tarnished diamond shape clock strikes 4 pm.

The House On Black Hill

Joshua is due to come home from work. His old Del laptop's screen shines once again, now that I turned it back on – it has been on standby for several hours.

The sky dresses a sick gray coat which frightens me : no clouds, no birds, no rain! Just an infinite steel color blanket. Wind starts to pick up speed, blowing furiously through the trees. I can hear its devilish howl when it scratches the tiles of the roof. The trees begin to dance angrily back and forth. Cold spikes run down my back because of it, and still, I am familiar with such wind.

I turn my head in both directions examining Joshua's old bedroom. His double bed covered with a floral quilt is pinned against the wall. The television sits in front of it on a newly cabinet. His mahogany wardrobe is right next to my desk. On the very right hand side is the window facing the main road, which leads to Madresfield.

Behind me, we have our own en suite, which means a real blessing. I try to search the internet for churches that specialize in exorcism or called more sophisticated : Deliverance ceremony.

This practice has not been used for, at least. 40 years. It could take months before we can get one approved. Downstairs, footsteps sounds and crumbled voices echo throughout the house. I focus on them, hoping to understand what the discussion is about. My attention gets caught when the laptop's screen brightens up and goes into the browser, then Google search bar - all by itself. I thought maybe a malware sneaked in the memory, but my hands reach for the keyboard and as if, I am guided by the unseen, I type about a ghost case from Romania. This story took place in Constanta and was popular between 2008-2009. It was about a woman that lived in a poor suburb area and who died aged 39 as a result of a heart attack. A week after she was buried, she returned as a vengeful spirit and haunted her family and even threatened them with death. Family claimed they have seen her, especially the children who would burst into tears at the sight of the vicious ghost. It was said that they tried she tried to steal money, gold jewellery and tempt the kids to follow her into death. The family tried desperately to get a cleansing done and an authorization to unbury her in order to get rid of the spirit. How it ended, remains a mystery to this day. Reporters have tried to reveal the strategy of the family on how they expelled the ghost- but despite their efforts; no one had a clue.

That intrigued me. Why am I shown this? Could this be

something similar? Jonathan Oswald could've been "needy" and tried to catch us, leading us to the other side?!

The headline of the article had demon written in it and that made me almost sick. Maybe if a catholic church won't help, maybe one of my belief will. I look up on the screen for an Orthodox church near me and the closest one is in Coventry. The distance didn't quite matter as long as I seek answers and help.

Meanwhile, Joshua creeps into the room with a warm plate of poached egg on toast. I remain silent writing down the address and details of the priest. Maybe we might go somewhere?...

Joshua calls my name, but half way through his sweet tone evaporates like steam. He places the plate next to me making me nearly jump, connecting me back to reality. I lift my head greeting his sapphire eyes. The color in his gaze has changed. Last time he got me here, he had hazel eyes, but now, they are bright blue again: - this is a sign that he is himself ; uncontrolled.

Joshua leans down so that he can steal a quick kiss. I smile as a welcome back. Then, his facial expression changes into shock. He faces the laptop screen while I begin eating. His eyes shine from the glow of the screen; and they are almost poisonous. Joshua's gaze comes back to me pumping with anger. At the top of the browser, the article remained open with the headline containing "demon", which is spelled exactly same in my language.

" Denisa, what is this? What is this shit?? Demon bla bla in your language?"

" Let me explain...It's not what it looks like.. Please calm down."

He throws himself onto the bed, pushing his hands behind his head.

" You got 5 minutes!"

" Look, if you translate it in English it will show you. It is a case similar to ours, that happened a few years ago. I heard of it when I was a teenager. I wanted to see of they found a solution, but...anyway I would like to go to an Orthodox church, and is in Coventry. Our priests are more open to this sort of stuff."

" And what makes you think that driving all the way to damn Coventry , will solve our problems?!"

That's it! His language, his attitude right now is the last drop I need on my pile of trouble.

" You know what?! Fine!!How will I know what Laura will

come up with? Might not be anything at all! If you don't take me, I will get there my damn-self."

Wind, outside, syncronizes with our tones. The atmosphere is too heavy. I can merely breath. My chest feels compressed. Joshua rubs his eyes with both palms, uncertain of what to do or say. He mumbles something I cannot understand.

" I am sorry..I am sorry I lashed out. I shouldn't have. I had a terrible day at work. Managed to get a few days break but had to listen to my manager's lecture."

" And...I will lose my job. How do you think Freya and Noah think about me?"

As I carry on eating, Joshua tries to translate the story to find out its content.

" Right...so you want me to take you to Coventry to see your own priest?!"

" Y-Yeah we have some cleansing ceremonies that might work."

" How are you feeling?"

" Better. I will take it easy."

With several attempts, I manage to reach Joshua and sit next to him on the bed. In the depth of my mind, I keep praying that God will protect us from this spirit,demon. Joshua glues me to his body. The warmth that comes from him, comforts me; shelters me from the outside world. I analyze his face and I see why his mother was worried. His skin color was returning in his cheeks. He used to be so pale and sick, like almost *dead...*

Chapter 12 Another sign

The same evening, around half past five , we are preparing the serve supper. As Martha lays the table, Joshua;s phone rings insanely, vibrating on the counter and shaking from the moves. He grabs it and moves a finger over the screen. A feminine voice greets him from the other end and didn't sound anyone familiar.

" Am I speaking to Joshua Sanders?"

" Yes, that is me. How can I help?"

" Hi there, I am Marina from Orbit Housing, I am afraid I have a complaint registered at your address!"

" A complaint about what? We are not even home, we are away for a couple of days."

" I see, how long you have been away for?"

" Been already 3-4 days."

" Right, I see. Well, might be worth checking to see if everything is ok. Neighbors on your floor have been complaining yesterday to our staff. They complained of bangs and heavy noises coming from apartment, especially at night time."

" I can reassure you it wasn't us, but we will go check as soon as possible. Sounds like something serious happened."

" I hope there is nothing serious and please let us know if we can help."

" Will do, thanks."

Joshua hangs up remaining frozen in the middle of the

kitchen. Martha looks for Maxwell, but the dog is nowhere to be found. He peers at me, shock reflecting in his eyes.

" What's wrong?" I ask worried.

" The council said our neighbors complained about hearing heavy noises from inside our apartment. We need to see what the hell is going on."

" Has anyone seen Maxwell? Dear can you go with you ? We can search for Maxwell, I hope he hasn't ran away."

Joshua and I decide to skip supper and make a move in his Ford. As I get in the car , an uneasy feeling starts to grow inside me. My heart sinks, this uneasiness grows painfully in my chest. I count the minutes which seem never-ending until we reach the apartment door. Joshua feel reluctant to even open the entrance door. We have been warned to stay away, but...something dragged us back.

Joshua brings her head against the wood, with one ear glued against the door, in attempt to listen if anything takes place inside. Then I can distinctly hear it too : - faint noises like rattling. Then, with few movements, the key jams and we enter the flat. Not long passes and Martha with Nathan join us. Everyone's faces change. Joshua is stunned; shock making him rigid. Martha covers her lips in surprise and Nathan appears surprised as well The entire place has been vandalized.

Our bedroom is cluttered. The cover from the bed and the pillows lie on the floor, torn paper like petals are spread all over the rugs. The kitchen cupboard doors are all wide open, revealing the contents. Our dining table is also trashed, few smashed glasses remain scattered on the floor, sparkling in the evening sunlight.

" This is not a break-in. The fucking door was locked!"

" It is that *thing !"*

My legs weaken and my throat turns dry; words refusing to articulate.

" How can somebody come in when the door is locked?" intervenes Nathan.

" I have told you there is something going on, but you didn't believe me."

I glance at Joshua. I watch him with terror and shock blend together. In my tries to run away, I cannot move. My body is still.; feels as if my feet are glued to the floor. Grabbing Joshua's hand I feel an ice carnal touch like someone dead's skin. The warmth has left him.

Alert, he says to me :

" We need to go to Coventry and fast!"

The House On Black Hill

Martha walks around the hallway examining the torn photographs and cracked glass from the picture frames.

" I need to go to bathroom, have a freshen up. I need to look for Maxwell."

" Darling, I am sure he will be fine. We will find him." Nathan follows Martha to the bathroom door tapping her shoulder gently as consolation. She puts on a faded, painful smile, then the door shuts. Joshua and me grab a few things for the trip, take a few pictures of the damages and decide to make a move when... Martha's sharp scream echoes throughout the flat. Then, extremely fast the bathroom door slams. Her shadow runs across the wall under the touch of the light and, after, it evaporates when the entrance door shuts brutally. Nathan chases her down the stairs wishing to calm her down.

The House On Black Hill

I go into the bathroom to see the cause of the scene. T my terror, the shape of a woman's head with ravaged face, who we have seen before, appears once more before my eyes; - but just as a leftover mist. She shown herself to my mother-in-law, scared her to death and now disperses like fog, revealing my reflection again.

" What happened?" yells Joshua.

" Your mom saw her...She saw that hideous woman in the mirror. Our apartment is trashed because of her."

Joshua examines his reflection for an instant and then grabs me by the shoulders. His grip makes me turn around and exit the flat. He locks the door while I stand behind him hopeless. I don't know what to do next. Everything we have tried has proved to be in vain. We have no control against this *demon.*

" Come on, let's get out of here. Let's go to Coventry!"

Joshua grabs my hand guiding me like a child. My mind is blank. I stare at the ground while my legs follow Joshua;s lead.. Next moment I sober again. The black Ford shines in the majestic remaining sunlight.

A male voice penetrates my ears , waking me up from this real nightmare.

" They've gone already. Let's hope Maxwell is alright."

" What-what next?"

" Get in the car Denisa. We are going to Coventry right now!"

Joshua's P.O.V.

Chapter 13 Not again

Between Denisa and I there is a intangible thin wall...Although I am driving; an unsettling silence is born. Not even the engine noise, the traffic murmur does not distract me. On the highway I can merely spot several cars coming our way or from the opposite direction. I get a split second to throw a rapid glance at her, to make sure she is alright. She seems distracted, detached from here...from *me.*

All these past 2 hours are a hell, her words are caged, she stops herself from speaking to me. It's killing me.

Coventry seems more like an after war city; the scruffy outskirts contain more ruins than inhabited buildings. The industrial estates we pass by, denote more untidiness and isolation. All the ground is bare: no vegetation dares to grow here. A few trees rise tall here and there in the weak sun, like standing soldiers. At the next junction we exit to a more quieter area. The street shrinks in the distance, becomes narrower and eerier. A few houses blended together as a chain, greet us. Finally, few life signs make themselves known: people going to the shop, a few chatting and one or two walking their dogs.

"How far is it till we reach the church?" I intrerupt Denisa.

" Hm...Not long now by the look of it. Bit down the road."

She turns her head to face me, her eyes appearing more alert. As soon as I stop the car, Denisa grabs my hand and guides me. Without looking around, she takes me to the church, as if she knew exactly the location and yet, this is the first time.

Past a narrow alley, I follow her without resisting. There are fences both sides, ready to squash us. At the end of the path, there it is - rising glamorously. The steel chapel sparkles under the touch of the poorly sun, the walls glow as well into a neat white. It's circular shape remind me of the mushroom houses from fairy tales.

" This is it, Joshua. Father Daniel should be there today."

Father Daniel? Father...Daniel....

My mind slides into a blackness, an infinite fog of nothingness.

The House On Black Hill

* * *

My phone begins to ring in my back pocket, making me aware of my surroundings once again. Denisa and I stop in front of the grandiose church, her puzzled look meeting me in same state of surprise. My mother is trying to get in touch with me. She has been trying to ring for the past minutes, but I slid into a different plane of mind.

As soon as I respond, mom's voice sounds terrorized:

"Joshua, thank goodness you answered...Oh dear, oh dear...Joshua...I.."

Her voice is trembling, I can feel the worry and anticipate she is crying at the other end. Her hiccups affect our conversation, sounding undecipherable.

"Calm down, please ! What happened? I don't get what are you saying."

She yells from the top of her voice mixed with cries in the phone:

"Maxwell is...DEAD! My furry baby is DEAD! Some bastard killed him."

"What?What? Where...Where did you find him?How Max got killed?"

"Somebody must've came into the house while we were with you..and killed him...oh dear,dear..."

From the other end, my father grabs the phone trying to reassure my mother. Soon, I hear his voice, a lot calmer then hers. Denisa watches me frozen.

"Joshua, when we came back from your apartment, we went into the hallway and found tracks of fur. Loads of fur scattered around the house like a trail, we thought Maxwell is losing his coat, but then we went upstairs to check on him..you know to feed him..and..we found blood stains and Maxwell was dead in the bathtub. We are still horrified, nothing is missing, just poor animal is lifeless. I can't explain this, but best for you to return as soon as possible. Meanwhile, please be careful!" and with this being said; our telephone discussion ends.

I place the phone back in the pocket and Denisa approaches me worried. I tell her what has happened with Maxwell, but her shock fades away, her eyes shining under the shadow of a tree. They show a seriousness and determination I have not seen before in her.

" So, that *thing* tries to scare us, to threat us. It is an awful sign that this demon or whatever it is, wants to destroy us. It has gone for poor Max – and it will come for us, too, if we don't stop it! We MUST stop it!"

" What makes you think it is the ghost?"

" Martha saw her in the mirror in our bathroom, she followed your mom back to the house. It went for Maxwell. He disappeared while we were at the apartment, then she saw her. Come on, Joshua it is so obvious! In my belief a vengeful spirit can kill and it usually begins with animals..."

For no reason, my heart pounds madly in my chest, almost making me sick. Her words stab me and shake my entire essence. I am aware of the gravity of the situation. If this entity could kill a dog, it can easily attack us. But blinded by pride, I refused to see it..or accept it; - until now.

Now, we are facing each other, stunned, still, trying to search for answers in each others' glace. Denisa points to the church, time seems to slow down. Crossing the road, hundreds of questions flood through my brain, but I am facing a blank wall as I don't know any of the answers. We enter the building. An immediate quietness greets us, the shy sunlight creeps in steadily. I admire the immense room covered in biblical scenes. All the intense, sharp colors come to life and feel like they take place before our eyes. So much false sensation of movement and, yet, when I look ahead, the room is empty.

At the far end, a few hanging pictures denote we are standing in a church. This is different from other churches I have attended in the past. The atmosphere in here is so peaceful; I haven't experienced it in a long time. All pictures hang on a detailed carved wall.

Denisa steps forward, her eyes searching for someone.

The House On Black Hill

Soft noises can be heard from behind the wall. As we get closer; they become distinct and louder. A man in a black robe with a bizarre hat salutes us. His beard and hair are slightly curly and steel-gray color. The lines on his face hide a painful story from many years ago. I can sense loneliness, but no sorrow. I believe he chose loneliness as an escape solution from something great which must've affected his life badly.

" Good afternoon, may I speak to Father Daniel,please?"

" I am Daniel. What can I do for you? I am afraid I cannot hold any ceremonies at this time."

"I am Denisa Sanders, I have sent you an email?"

"Oh yes. Please have a seat." Once we sit down at the back of the church, the priest crosses his hands, all ready to listen to us. Denisa's tone shakes from despair, she can't get the wording right.

" My husband is English, so I need to explain in my mother tongue".

I nod my head in approval and next thing I witness two people speaking in front of me in a different language and I listen like a rag doll sat on a shelf. I understand the word *demon,* being mentioned several times. I can assume it is the entity that torments us.

The priest turns to me and glances at me, wise and serious waves building in his ocular pearls.

"Joshua" he tries to open the discussion with a soft, still very deep man voice. His accent is so tough. " I have spoken with Denisa and you two must have a house cleansing act . I can perform that, but I need to prepare for it , which includes fasting on Wednesday and Friday. I can perform it on the 15 August when it is a holy day."

It is nearly a month, but he said he will do it.

" And what if this demon attacks us during this time? What do you suggest then?"

He grabs from a cabinet nearby, a wood box and hands it over to me, pointing at what the contents are.

" I have already told Denisa about it. This is blessed incense from 40 masses. Burn this and smudge the house, put holy water on the corner of the doors and read psalm 23 from the Bible. This should be sufficient until I do the ceremony"

As soon as I grab the box, I feel sudden anger rising within me. My blood boils at this point and my hand shakes madly. I shudder knowing it is not me anymore. I try to call Denisa, to make her run, but words are stuck in my throat. The box ends on the floor. I can feel myself standing and jumping at my wife. Denisa steps back, finding herself pinned against the wall. The priest's face is consumed by fear as he murmurs a prayer. It is as if I look in a mirror and see my own reflection doing its own actions. Denisa's shock and terror can be read on her face. I scream her name, but she can't hear me.

<<*She can't hear you any longer...ha ha ha*>>

You!! Get the fuck out of my head! If you hurt her I swear to God, I will send you to Hell, where you belong!

Tears fall down her cheeks, glowing in the dull sunlight. She gasps, begging me, calling my name. I stand in front of her intimidatingly, fixating her with anger filled eyes. As I grab her by the shoulders, she shudders under my grip. Then, slowly, my hands move up targeting her neck, but for a brief moment we are both paralyzed.

My hands refuse to move. Suddenly, they start to shake brutally and, then a burning sensation invades me. *What is going on?*

The priest comes between us and throws some smelly liquid on me. I fall on my knees, my whole body burning, but feeling like I gather control again. Everything surrounding me becomes sober and alert. Denisa's yelling penetrates my ears. Her calling out my name, brings involuntary tears into my eyes.

I was manipulated. This thing wanted me to strangle my wife.

" D-Denisa, I am so sorry...Please forgive me. It wasn't me...It was that entity, I swear...I swear to God...I would never dare to hurt you."

Grave silence...This silence stabs me deeper than a blade. Denisa supports herself using the chair. She keeps a serious distance from me, her scared gaze hides from me as I still remain rigid trying to pull myself together. The priest taps me on the shoulder repeating insanely : " It is ok, it is ok."

No! It's not dammit ok!

" You will be fine, Joshua. I have thrown a special blessed water over you. You were possessed...I need t-to prepare for the cleansing. Please take this." He gives the box that caused the trouble in the first place. Denisa refuses to get anywhere near me. Father Daniel shows a smile as a confirmation that everything is safe. I just wipe my face and get out of the building cowardly. My whole world trembles, feels like the ground loses stability beneath my feet, I am sick with worry, and sick of this shit! So sick - that death appears a tempting solution.

I glue my back on the tree close by to the church, just across the street. My bloods pumps angrily and perspiration flows down my temples like small streams.

Denisa arrives after, her despair melt away. I see again same worry in her eyes , my mother had. I instinctively grab her left hand, turning round so that we swap places; her pinned against the tree trunk and me in front of her. I can't do the same mistake, just can't.

I can reassure her it's me, that she is secure with me. My lips reach for hers forming a light kiss. A shock units us and brings us closer.

" I thought we will die..."

" I am not letting any fucking entity win this battle. I promise..."

Chapter 14 : I am scared...

Denisa breaks the second kiss and with both her hands, she pushes me away. Her body moves farther from me as if she is a scared child. The expression on her face changes once more. I meet the same fearful eyes; same ones I am becoming more and more used to lately. I am petrified of the idea that now she starts being afraid of me, that she doesn't feel safe by my side anymore; that maybe, like earlier, I might break out and do something idiotic.

" Joshua, please stay away from me. I will go home by train, or-or I will take a taxi."

" You what? Take a train? We came here together and we

leave together!"

" No! I am afraid of you. YOU TRIED TO KILL ME" she shouts almost disturbing the afternoon's public peace.

Her voice hammers in my head, causing me headache. It's a painful reminder to what has just happened.

" I am serious. Stay away from me."

" Come on Denisa. For crying out loud, I am sorry. I didn't mean to."

" You tried to fucking grab me by my throat, Joshua! What guarantee I have that you will not try it again!?"

I am speechless. My mind goes blank and I, just get so confused. A heavy weight seems to push down my chest, I feel like I am suffocating. I just can't describe the pain. Denisa turns her back on me, occasionally raising her hand to wipe the tears away. I stand in the middle of nowhere not knowing what to do. I want to chase and grab her, drag her to the car and forget this nonsense for a moment, but something tells me she might cause a scene.

The tree trembles because of my repetitive kicks. Probably feels same tremble I do inside. Frustration invades me...Denisa's presence fades away behind some buildings; away from me, away from my madness. My ration kicks me violently. I try to catch up with her, the pace of my steps quicken so that, in the end, I reach her. She refuses to have eye contact, and to be honest, I don't blame her.

She avoids me and follows the signs to the train station. My blood boils at this point. I just cut in front of her; I have been doing enough the obeying puppy behavior.

" Denisa, where are you going?"

" Isn't it obvious? To the train station."

I just can't hold it, I pull her by the elbow and we are inches apart from each other. The fabric of her blue shirt brushes over my denim jacket.

" Just, let me go! I really had enough of this. Please!"

" I love you, just...just come with me in the car. You can sit in the back, opposite me. Come on, just – let's go home!"

This pathetic declaration manages to make her drop her guard. But, I still feel the bitterness in her moves and the acid tone she speaks to me. In the car, we remain silent. The trip back home proves slower and painful than before... I experience mixed feelings. Her words : *I am scared of you,* classify me as a monster.

Chapter 15 : *The house is the grudge*

While we are stopping by at the services station for a break, both mobile phones go off. Although, curiosity pushes me, in the end, I just abandon the idea. Denisa has no interest in me or dares to talk to me. The gravity of the situation upsets me deeply. But, I cannot do much until we return to Malvern.

* * *

Returned to the flat and exhausted, I unlock the front door. Denisa and I face an unwelcoming and trashed apartment. Since we left, everything remained scattered everywhere. I closed the cupboard doors again and tidied up the kitchen, while my wife sorted out the bedroom and bathroom. Without any energy left, I excuse myself for supper and head to bed. I ask Denisa if she wants me to sleep on the couch or lie on the bed. She nods for me to have a rest in our bedroom. She finishes her supper as I return to bed. Our conversation is been plain: *bitter* and *plain*. I don't really dare to bring back the topic of what has happened. I cannot stand another fight.

I throw myself on the bed with my arms wide open, starring at the ceiling. My marriage has been ruined by something I never believed in. An unnatural force had brought so much darkness and damage into our lives that now it seems that maybe it is succeeding. The love temple and respect we have built, now falls into decay. The harmonious life we established, goes down the plug hole; it is ruined in an instant 'cause of this *thing.*

I turn my head towards Denisa's side of the bed. Her phone was left to charge and it was lighting up. I turn to fetch it and see what is going on with it. An envelope flashes on the screen with the name: Laura Martnen and below a few other unread emails from work. Without realizing I check through them and find out that this medium asked how we are and wanted to perform another clearing ceremony, few of the other emails were from Denisa's manager asking when she will go back to work, to explain her behavior and that she must get in touch as soon as possible. The fact which amazes me is that she didn't bother; she has always been so organized and now, she has has lost interest. I feel guilty for not being more closer and supportive. I ran away once, or twice, can't do it again. Running is not an option! I have to stay and protect her, she has only myself.

I do not notice when Denisa starts saying a prayer in the kitchen, well, sounds like it to me. I think for a moment, maybe is her way to cope with things, hoping to bring some peace and balance. Listening to her whisper pushes me into a leisure state of mind. I drift to sleep sitting awkwardly onto the bed. I can still hear her voice in the distance. Then; she vanishes.

I can see myself on top of her, with my hands aiming at her neck again. She fights me, kicks me but that doesn't make me budge.

What is going on?

Her screams make me laugh with passion. It is a joy to see her struggle. Somehow, I witness how I torture my own wife. I am horrified.

What the fuck? This is not me? It's you! Leave Denisa alone! I love her...I would never ever hurt her...Please God...NO!

I see myself stopping. Denisa grabs a crucifix and hits me with it, making me fall on the floor unconscious. Once more, the burning sensation comes back and I wake up sweating. My eyes widen, perspiration covers my face and my hands. My heart races and the sweet whispers continue to raise from the kitchen. Denisa is still praying and burning that incense Father Daniel gave her.

Was I dreaming? Or was I seeing a premonition?

I get off the bed and creep outside the bedroom. Silently, I watch Denisa sat at the table with the Bible in front of her and relaxed. Arriving in the kitchen, she senses my presence and lifts her head . She glances at me; a thin smile rising in the corner of her lips. A smile. This is what I need. I collapse at her feet and she questions me. But, I place my head on her lap trying to hide the sadness and worry that read in my eyes. She touches my hair gently. I can tell she is not afraid this time.

" I love you."

" I love you too, Joshua."

Denisa raises my head and cups both of my cheeks. Her face leans down to kiss me. Our lips unite passionately. My entire face is burning, but not from anger, it is desire and love. I am getting the power back. My phone rings and I reach to see the reason. No call just a blank message which looks familiar. I show it to my wife and we both are astonished.

" This is the message I got that day at the quarry:

The grudge is not in the house, the house is the grudge."

Chapter 16 : The house is the grudge II

My eyes widen as soon as I recognize the message. "The house...the house..the house on Black Hill."

Staring at the phone, a wave of questions raises in my head. The screen turns black again as if nothing happened. I blink at it before turning my head back to Denisa. Our kitchen lapses in silence. Something hard stops me from swallowing. I try to force the words out, but in vain. My throat is so dry. Pressing my hand to my temple, a lance of pain strikes, almost making me lose my balance.

" I never got that message. It was always you. I think I understand... The entity wanted you, it used you to get to me."

says Denisa with a soft tone.

The pain in my head fragments, closing my eyes in an effort to gather myself together. In the last two days, I have experienced a flood of mixed feelings: from love to hate, from fear to courage, from fright to ambition. All blended together left me hanging in uncertainty. I just want all of this to end.

" Joshua that house..."

That house, that house...

Denisa's voice disperses like smoke, my inner voice repeating insanely the word "house".

Yes! That's right! It is where everything started. All this began when we went to that fucking house on Black Hill. - and that's where it has to END.

My wife's hand taps one of my shoulders and I turn to her

again. Seeing her face lifts up my spirits.

" What is that thing called which you were burning?"

" It is a strong incense from the church. The smoke is effective against all spirits."

" I do feel better. Do you think it worked?"

She nods smiling at the same time. This represents a big reassurance for me. Indeed, everything seems peaceful – still and peaceful. The heaviness from the air has vanished and, for the first time, in months, we feel relieved. - I feel released.

Denisa's eyes battle with leftover fear and joy.

" Listen Denisa..." I grab her hands and rub them with my fingers in an attempt to comfort her. " I'm here, I am Joshua you married and you love. I will never hurt you. Those evil thoughts were coming from that entity. I would never think about anything like that."

" I know you wouldn't." she speaks so sweet while caressing my hair.

Like a thunder, a stream of wisdom strikes my brain. I step away from Denisa, while her puzzled look fixates my body.

" I know you were right. I think I know how to sort stuff out."

Banging my fists together, her response comes as silence and confusion.

" If we take some of that incense, we can do a cleansing ourselves up there, Denisa. Cleanse that fucking house on Black Hill! Worth a shot, what do you say?"

Suddenly, she starts laughing rubbing her tired eyes.

" Wow, been a long time since you came up with an idea! Usually I do the thinking."

" Very funny darling. Let's go before weather gets worse."

Denisa and I leave the apartment somehow excited. We

found a solution ourselves that might work, or not, but we decided to take manner into our own hands. Laura Martnen's medium abilities have made things worse, Reverend Mathias never got back to us. The only priest who really showed some compassion was Father Daniel. From all these people, he is the only one who stood by our side and whatever secret ace he had; he supported me in finding myself again.

I unlock the black Ford by pressing the key, making the headlights flicker.

I'm gonna tear that fucking house down.

Denisa gets in the passenger seat and I get behind the wheel. Starting the engine, my brain storms with possibilities.

What else can I lose?

Leaving the parking space, I meditate on my moves. Denisa is lost in her own thoughts. My glance returns from time to time to the rear mirror, remembering that day when Jonathan Oswald's ghost was sat in the back of the car. There is no other presence except us in the vehicle. Above, the clouds were beginning to gather like soldiers.

My cheeks burn from a wave of rage. *So if smudge, smoke...in other words, smoke comes from fire..Yes, fire has to be the answer!*

On the street, there is a great and rather strange silence. The noon and apparently miserable weather forces everyone to stay indoors.

I decide to stop at the gas station for a fuel top up. Denisa continues to watch out the window contemplating perhaps on the the disgraceful weather. She probably questions my intentions. Pumping the fuel in the Ford, I get invaded by a disturbing vision. The face of Jonathan Oswald stares at me with same wasted face full of burgundy stains . His laughter remains mute, but all I glance at, is his black toothless mouth. A horn beeping in the distance brings me back to reality. Another vehicle passes by with windows wide open. The driver waves at me like mad. It is Jamie, the Irish coworker.

Stood rigid and smiling, I manage to wave back at him holding the fuel pump with my other hand. An idea roots drastically, my heart hammers so strong; I can almost heart its rhythm.

Petrol, lighter...fire... That's it old man, or fucking demon. I had enough of this.

After finishing putting the fuel in, I grab the canister from the trunk and fill that too. As I head to the counter I make my plan in my head. I have everything I need. Thrilled with my decision I return to the car once I paid. Driving to Black Hill's parking lot, I focus on the steps I must follow. How will I explain to Denisa that carrying this petrol canister will be the final step, ultimate gesture to end up this nightmare?

Reaching the bottom of the hill, terror glows in Denisa's eyes. She appears to be afraid to speak. Probably wonders what the hell I am doing. To make sure, she doesn't get suspicious I offer to go last.

My words panic her. With both hands she locks all the doors, leaving me outside. I bang against the windows screaming her name.

" What the hell you think you are doing with that canister? Don't think I didn't see you. What was your sick plan, huh? To set the car, to set me on fire?"

My jaw drops. *How she can believe this? Does she think I am that sick-minded?*

The House On Black Hill

" I had a feeling something was fishy. I saw it on your damn face, Joshua. All that bull-crap talking was to get me out of the house..I thought for a second you are normal again!"

I hesitate to answer, swallowing becomes so difficult. Her eyes flick rapidly from side to side.

" I'm gonna call the police!"

" Denisa, no! You don't understand I'd never dare to...that petrol was meant to be for the house. I-I wanted you to go a different way and I would go up the hill and set that fucking house on fire!" my words shake violently.

She stops fixating me with tearful eyes. My own vision blurs. I touch the chilled glass with my forehead. Her muffled voice coming from inside paralyzes me and leaves me cold.

" I swear I wanted to see that damn house burn down to ashes!"

The window on her side slides down a few inches, enough to hear her voice clearer.

" If so, I am not going up there. I want you to step away and I will run from the car. You stay away, don't come looking for me."

I follow her instructions, feeling torn in two as I do this. I never felt so empty and incomplete; to lose the trust of the person I love dearly.

Once the passenger door opens, Denisa gets out and runs like a frightened rabbit. For a second , I doubt my plan. Maybe this actually made it worse.

How foolish to believe that I can solve our problems.

Behind me, the wind moves through the woods. The trees swing from the violent hit. Few dead leaves dance across the ground, patting my feet in their walk. I look at the horizon and realize it is darker than before. The storm is coming...

Unable to walk, I stare at nothing. A familiar laughter penetrates my ears. I cover them and look behind me, facing same evil grin that makes fun of me. It is her; that hideous woman! Her mutilated face scratched or burnt builds a smirk; thrilled from the earlier scene she assisted to.

My gaze changes, anger grows within me and my fists tremble from fury. I am aware of my rapid breathing. I almost feel the need to gag. Her scent of decay, of rotting flesh invades my nostrils, and the discusting flavor of decomposing , almost touches my tongue. I can just about taste it!

Fucking had enough of this.

I close my eyes praying. I inhale a mouthful of fresh air and search the glove compartment in the car. She was gone, I think to myself. Denisa's incense and the lighter were left in the compartment. Reaching for the canister, I lock the car and climb the Black Hill. Perspiration drop flow down my face and my entire body is on fire. My legs feel so heavy, but my determination has to be stronger. Time seems to drag, for an instant the clouds stop moving . Everything is stiff.

Although, the wind tries to push me, I make my way past the obstacles. Reaching at the far end of the hill, I can see the roof of the house hiding in the woods.

This is it.

Getting closer and closer, screams can he heard louder and clearer. They lurk inside the house. A variety of dreadful yells as if a whole crowd of people suffering simultaneously, echos throughout the forest.

Perhaps house screams for salvation...or the souls from inside do.

The House On Black Hill

Indeed, the house is the grudge. Unscrewing the cap, I throw the incense inside the canister and circle the house, spilling the petrol all over the walls and foundation. Nor the screams, nor the banging in the windows will put an end to my actions.

The canister falls aside and with both hands shaking repetitively, I light the lighter. The sound of friction amplifies behind me, and with that so does the emptiness. I lean down to release the flame and immediately it sparkles. It doesn't take long until the flames grow angrily, swallowing the building. Black smoke flies in the sky and once again clouds gather monstrously fast. All the screams evaporate as the house hides in the flames. I can no longer recognize the surroundings.

I fall on the grass gasping for air. The heaviness from my

shoulders has been taken away. I feel so free, so released. The scent of smoke and incense burning together bring a smile on my face.

Maybe this is it?!

The end of the house on Black Hill.

Denisa's P.O.V.

Chapter 17 The final

" Joshua! Joshua!"

The air leaves my lungs. Above the trees, the layer of smoke swallows the landscape. My heart races and I burst into tears knowing who is responsible. All the voices in my head force me to yell his name and run back on Black Hill. Wind picks up wiping my tears away. Breathless I try to climb over the steep stones to get to Joshua. The black blanket above me warms me of the storm approaching. I ache all over, pain strikes me in my legs, but will not give up. The sky watches me, I feel so. Taking a dangerous turn towards the bushes , I spot Joshua sat up in grass.

" Joshua!"

   Through the thick cloud of smoke I can merely make out the remains of the roof. Bit by bit it begins to collapse. Joshua stands up and runs towards me. He wraps his arms around me tightly while I squeeze his shirt with my fists. He strokes my hair, then kisses it gently.

" You are back. But-but why?"

" I saw the smoke and I thought..I thought you've done something stupid."

He giggles at my afirmation. Like waking from a dream, I lift my head grabbing his cheeks and offering an intense kiss on his lips. They're rough and taste like smoke.

   Out of the blue, cold tears fall down from the sky, the pace rapidly increases as we head back down to the car.

Throwing the canister in the back, we climb into the vehicle soaking wet. It feels different. The layer of silence and distance between us vanishes.

" I'm so sorry."

" I know, me too. Sorry for the odd behavior. Better ring the firemen."

Joshua drives off while I phone for the firefighters. Of course, meanwhile both of us witness the thunder hitting on Black Hill a few times in the same spot. I believe it is not a coincidence.

EPILOGUE

Two days later, Laura Martnen returned to our apartment for a visit. She wore a denim suit with floral shirt and freed hair. She is professional as usual. In between, her face turned thinner, consumed by the challenges she occurred with this living nightmare.

Shocked, she looked around the flat searching for something.

" I can't feel anything, apart from peace" she said smiling.

We sat together around the coffee table. She crossed her legs and reached for her cup. After taking a sip, Laura raised her eyebrows.

" Well, I have a question for you two."

She gets something out of her hand bag, something like a newspaper. It was the local gazette. The headline caught my eye instantly:

<< *Mysterious house on Black Hill devastated by fire*>>

" *Firefighters find ruins and ashes at the scene. Locals witnessed lightning striking multiple times up the hills. The fire was put off, but how caused it, remains unknown. Police considers maybe a reckless walker's cigarette bud could have started the fire as well as a natural disaster.*

** *Fourtunately, no one was harmed and the house appears to have been empty for a long time.*"**

" I have a feeling you to have something to do with this. This is the reason I came to see you. Anyway, it looks like that fire eradicated the evil and purified the place. I must say it is a

miracle. Congratulations."

Laura remained a close friend of ours. Joshua returned to work changed as a more open-minded person. Our relationship has become stronger. Martha and Nathan opened their minds as well to the forces of unseen, and started going to church more often.

I...well I gave up my old job at Brendon House. I could not bare to see more residents passing away. Had enough of death! I managed to find a job as a sales assistant in a nearby shop. As for our old apartment, we gave it back to Orbit Housing. We moved to a one bedroom house outside Malvern. That apartment hold too many painful memories to keep living in it. And I hope I never have to hear about Black Hill again...

The House On Black Hill

Printed in Great Britain
by Amazon